Palace Center

Frida Collins

Contents

1

Riyang pov -

It was a rainy night when everything changed. My innocence was taken from me at thirteen years old by a man twice my age. It wasn't easy after that, having to walk around as if I was cursed to bring misfortune upon the whole city. My son was worth the pain I went through, seeing him so beautiful and innocent in this ugly and evil world.

After he was born, my family disowned me, saying it was my fault that a man touched me and found me worthless. I was forced to live on the streets, begging and working for food. That's when I met her.

I thought she would make my life better. She brought me to a warm house and gave me a nice scrub. She dressed me up prettily and told me I shouldn't suffer any longer and should be paid to have men beg for me. I listened to her and suffered the price.

My son was raised in a brothel, alongside his half brother, who I hid from Mistress. My sisters were very helpful with my children, which I was thankful for. But I hated the life that had been forced upon me.

"Mama, I miss you a lot." I looked down and smiled at the young man before me, his appearance tall and proud despite his hardships. His younger brother smiled beside him, also happy as I laid my eyes upon the two of them.

"I'm sorry, my lovely children. I dislike being away from you. But I have to feed you and your large appetites somehow." I replied, ruffling their hair. I loved the feeling of their soft curls since it brought me so much peace.

"I understand mama. But I wish I could go to school as the other children do." The younger do the two said, pouting and giving me his best-begging face. I chuckled and pinched his cheeks.

"You're already smarter than the rest, why show off?" I asked, making him sigh.

"Rui ge, take me to school too." He asked, making the elder laugh.

"But Xiaoyang, you already know the same amount of letters and numbers as any palace official would since our mother is very smart and knows all the words to be known in the capital." He replied, making the younger pout again.

"Boys, my beautiful and smart sons, let's eat some dinner, hmm?" I stated, ending the conversation and bringing out some beef and rice.

I wished they would always be this innocent and happy. Watching them laugh and talk to each other about anything and everything gave me the most happiness I could ever receive from anyone. But it was always short-lived.

A single knock on the door would indicate that Mistress was coming to check on us. A single knock meant the boys must hide and evidence of their living as quickly as possible. It was hard, teaching them and making them live that way, but it had to be done. They could be killed for just breathing if they were caught.

"Good evening, my lovely Riyang. How was your day?" She asked, a sly smile upon her colored lips as she sat in front of me, examining my movements.

"Fine, sister. Do you have another client for me?" I replied, smiling as I offered her tea.

"Yes. He is on his way now. Paid quite a high price to see you. I told you that you were worth much." She replied, drinking the warm liquid with a smile.

"How much was it?" I asked, hoping to earn some coin to buy some cloth.

"Five hundred pieces of silver." She answered, making me gasp.

"Five hundred? I've never had that much of a price before. Is he of a higher rank than usual?" I questioned, earning a nod as she giggled.

"Treat him well, darling. I'll reward you with a bigger room." She told me, giving me one last look of determination before leaving.

- Mingrui pov -

"Rui ge I don't think we should go in there." I looked at my brother with a smirk.

"But think of all the treasure we could find. We can buy our mother her freedom!" I explained, earning a look of consideration as he contemplated his options.

"That's a good idea I guess. But what if we get caught? We could be killed." He replied, making me roll my eyes.

"Stop thinking so negatively Shuyang, we can do this!" I told him, taking his hand and leading him in through the small alleyway that would lead to the expensive house I'd seen last time I went exploring.

I knew stealing was wrong, but what my mother was being forced to go through was much worse than a few pieces of jade missing from an old house that no one lived in.

I picked up a few pieces with a smile, knowing I could save my mother from her life with these valuable gems. But that happiness didn't last long as my hand was snatched in mid-air, a strong grip upon my wrist as I was pulled out of the building.

"You're hurting me!" I whined, making the man chuckle.

"You're committing a crime worthy of death, and you're complaining about pain?" He stated, making me shut my mouth as I was shoved to the ground alongside my brother.

"I told you we shouldn't have come here. Mama is going to kill us." Shuyang whispered, making me roll my eyes.

"What is your mother's name?" The man asked, his eyes glaring at us as we didn't respond. "I could kill you now and send you to an unmarked grave, but I'm sure you'd rather be buried in your family plot."

"We don't have a family plot." I shoved Shuyang as he spoke up, making him confused. "Mama taught us to respect the officials of the palace."

"She taught you well, but it seems as though your brother as different plans. Maybe I should teach him a lesson on respecting his elders." The man stated, smiling at me as he grabbed a pole.

2

Riyang pov -

I stormed into the court with a wave of fuming anger as I walked towards to hall my sons were being held.

"Mama!" I looked at the younger with a look of anger, making him pause in his running towards me.

"Shuyang, what did I tell you about leaving the house?" I asked, making him how his head in shame. A man came up to me with a glare.

"Fang Riyang?" I nodded and he handed me a paper listing the things the children took. "You will have to talk to the emperor himself about the jade stolen from the Queen's residence."

"You went to the Queen's residence?" I questioned, making the child fall to the floor.

"Mingrui ge wanted to save you from your life and brought me through the alley to the house. I didn't know anything, mama. I'm sorry." He cried, whimpering as the man grabbed him.

"Where is his brother?" I asked, making the man sigh.

"He showed the boss a bit of attitude, so he was whipped. He's lying in the other room, healing." He answered, pointing his head in the direction of my child.

I took Shuyang and ran to the room, letting out a sudden sob when I saw my child, bloody and unconscious upon the bed.

"Why must you be so bold, Mingrui, my son?" I asked, holding his head as I washed his wounds. "Why did you want to rescue me so much that you took this risk?"

"My lady, if I may ask, what is your occupation? Your dress appears to be one of a consort." The man asked as he entered the room.

"You have guessed correctly, my Lord. I am a woman from the House of Petals Brothel." I replied, sighing as I looked to the ground in shame. "My children are a secret, and I know I raised them wrongly in this manner. My apologies, my Lord."

"Come tomorrow, and you can pick up your children after speaking with the emperor." He softly said, feeling sorry that he had to do his job. I nodded and smiled, trying to hide my tears from my younger son as I hugged him.

"Be good, okay? I'll be back tomorrow. Take care of your brother." I softly said, ruffling his hair and smiling fondly at him before taking my leave.

As soon as I left, I dropped to the ground in tears, knowing that we could all die for my son's careless actions. I loved them dearly, and the thought behind the action was a worthy one, but he did it the wrong way, and we'll have to pay the price somehow. I prayed the king would be generous and kind to us.

- Shuyang pov -

I flinched when my brother moaned in pain. I stopped cleaning his wound and looked at his face, sobbing as he made eye contact with me.

"Gege, I'm so scared," I whispered, making him groan as he turned his head, examining our surroundings.

"How long was I asleep?" He asked, wincing as he sat up.

"A few hours now. Mama stopped by. She has to talk to the emperor and beg for us to live after stealing the Queen's jade pieces." I replied, making him chuckle.

"We're in the palace? That's interesting." He answered, making me groan with frustration. "What? It's a really fun experience even if we won't live to remember it."

"Gege I don't want to die!" I shouted, making him look to me with his round eyes. "I'm scared and you're taking this whole thing as if it was a fun game!"

"It's time." I flinched as the guard came in again, giving us a soft but firm look as he waited for us to follow him out of the room.

I carried Mingrui on my side, helping him limp down the hall towards the courtyard where we would stand trial. I was frightened for my life, but I put on the best face I could as I made eye contact with my mother, who was sobbing crazily as we came into view.

"Mama, what's wrong?" I softly asked, waiting for her reply as we were placed beside her. She held us close and looked to the man on the throne with a fiery glare.

"You cannot take my sons away from me. I will not let you." She stated, cold and calm as she held our hands tightly.

"I can kill you and take them anyways." He replied, making me whimper as his cold eyes stared into my own. "Which one of them is the elder?"

"The one that was beaten to near-death by your guards." Mama spat, still glaring at the man in the throne as he looked to his guards with anger.

"You dare hurt a son of the throne? Where is the one that beat him? I'll have his head." I looked to Mama in confusion as Mingrui mirrored my action.

"What does he mean?" Mingrui asked, stuttering as she looked to the ground.

"He means that he is your father, Mingrui. You're a prince, my son." She softly said, pain flooding from her lips as she held us close.

I watched as my brother fell to the ground in shock, unable to process how the man before us was my brother's father. He looked old enough to be our mother's father. It didn't make sense to me at all.

"I can see you are all a little shocked. As my son, he will reside in the palace from now on. He will learn from his elder brothers on how to behave and become a strong man." He said, making my heart clench. I stood up and faced him with a face of determination as I locked eyes with him.

"You, you will not take my brother away from me," I said, firm in my stance but my words shaky with fear. My mother grabbed my hand, but I shook her off, wanting to do this on my own. "He is my blood. You will not take him."

3

I watched in shock as my younger son stood up to the emperor. The one I'd always thought to be shy and humble was now standing as if he was the only man on Earth, and was unwilling to back down to anyone.

After the young man nearly spat at the ruler, the old man just laughed, slapping his hand upon his throne.

"I will take your brother, young man, and I will raise him as the royal he is meant to be. You can be his servant if you like. I'll allow you to reside with him so as to not leave your side as you requested." He stated, making me let out a breath of relief.

"Will you free my mother as well?" Shuyang asked, earning a chuckle and a nod.

"From now on, she will no longer be a concubine for the public to use. She will solely be for the Royal Family. She will reside here alongside the other women and their children." The elder answered, making me want to run away.

The palace was generous, yes, but it was a deadly place to live, and even worse if one had a life like mine. If I was bound to be trapped in here, I knew I would not live a long and happy life.

"I want her to be free. Not just another wife for you or your sons to ignore for years on end." Shuyang stated, earning a gasp from some of the guards.

"How dare you raise your voice to the emperor. Do you want to die?" The closest one said, pulling his sword from its holster. I jumped in front of my son, glaring at the man before me.

"If you touch my son I will not hesitate to kill you," I told him, making him laugh.

"A woman like you? You can't do anything except please men like me." He growled, only stopping as the king held his hand up. The guard returned to his place and placed his sword back into the sheath.

"I admire your bravery, young lady. And to your son as well. I will allow you to live in the palace as a court lady. No one will touch you at all, until I change my mind on the matter." He announced, making his men bow and move to take me, Shuyang, and our belongings to our new house within the palace walls.

I cried as we were placed inside a building that was much more detailed and expensive than the one we had known. Shuyang looked to me with a face of confusion, unsure if I was happy or saddened by the new arrangements.

I ruffled his hair and hugged him tightly. I couldn't bear to lose him as well. I knew Mingrui would be raised as a strong man, but I feared for his life, knowing that princes had a habit of fighting for the throne and killing one another for a chance to sit on the seat they all crave.

- Yuan pov -

I walked over to where I heard the screaming. I saw my father laughing as a young boy stood in front of his beaten mother and brother with determination. I chuckled as he resembled my brother, knowing he didn't have any children that were that old.

I watched the scene unfold as he demanded a place for his mother that would be freeing from her position as a concubine. I truly didn't pay attention to his words until Father said the beaten boy would be raised as my younger sibling.

After the two were dragged away, I walked over into view and bowed to my father.

"I'm sorry, your majesty, but I couldn't help but overhear this conversation. This boy here," I paused to look at the weak boy who was still bruised and bloody, giving him a pitiful stare. "This boy is my brother?"

"Yes. He is your brother. Please raise him as such." He replied, making both me and the younger gulp with nervous anticipation.

I led him to my residence since he didn't have a room of his own yet. I smiled as my brother joined me, looking upon the child with confusion as I had.

"Xing Ge this is our little brother, Xiaorui," I said, making the elder show off his dimples as he smiled, greeting the young boy as if he'd known him his whole life.

"Xiaorui, nice to meet you. I'd heard Father had a Mistress somewhere. Good to know I have a second brother to care for." He softly said, holding out his hand as a greeting.

I let out a laugh as the boy shoved the hand away and pouted, crossing his arms and slamming himself to the floor in an outburst of anger.

"I don't care who either of you are. I want to see my mother and stay with her." He demanded, making Yixing and I laugh.

"I'm sure she'll be given permission to visit you eventually. For now, though, pretend my mother is yours. She will take care of you as if you were her son." I told him, earning a harsh glare I didn't know was possible on such a young and adorable child.

"I can see why the guard beat you, you have such a temper," Yixing said, making the younger flinch as I chuckled. "Don't worry, you don't have to fear that again now that you are known to be a prince. Anyone who touches you with evil intent will be put to death."

"I miss my brother." He pouted, trying to remain in a tough appearance as his tears slipped from his eyes. "We've never been apart. I need to see him."

"Tomorrow. You can see your brother and your other tomorrow. I'll help you greet them after you've had some rest to treat your wounds." I replied, ruffling his hair as he looked around sleepily. "Go to sleep, Mingrui. We'll see them tomorrow."

"I'll go with you. I want to see why his mother got so much attention from Father, enough to have the right to bear his child without anyone knowing about it until now." Yixing whispered so as to not wake the sleeping child. I nodded and smiled, hoping to see the woman in a better appearance than what was shown this morning.

4

Riyang pov -

I sighed with irritation at the servants who dressed me up in order to greet the princes that were to arrive later today. I disliked the fancy clothes given to me as if I was a doll for others to praise.

"Mama look at how fancy my Hanfu is! I've never had such pretty clothes!" I smiled as Shuyang came running in, showing off his beautiful dress and adorable smile as he hugged me. "I know you dislike it here as well, but we'll be together and fed now. You don't have to worry as much."

"I thank the heavens for giving me a son like you, my dear Shuyang. Please grow into a nice young man, stay brilliant and shining." I softly said, holding my breath as the door was opened, revealing a face I had forgotten about following closely behind my elder son.

We made eye contact and he stopped in his tracks, looking at me, Mingrui, and Shuyang. The other man beside him was confused, looking between the two of us for an answer.

"Ri, Riyang?" He stuttered out, making me back away from him.

"You, you were a prince?" I asked, holding Shuyang close as I found myself backing up until I couldn't go any farther.

"You know each other?" The other asked, earning a nod from both of us.

"When we were fourteen, Father sent me to find a wife. You remember that, don't you Yuan?" Yixing stated, earning a nod. "I met Riyang and fell in love with her. Father wouldn't allow me to marry her, though, since she was a consort at a brothel."

"But you made sure to leave behind a lasting memory in that poor girl's mind, didn't you?" Yuan asked, looking at Shuyang as I held him.

"Is, is he my father?" The small boy asked, turning around and looking at me for an answer. I nodded unwillingly, looking away to watch Yixing as he fell to his knees.

"I, I didn't know. If I did, I would've helped you become free a long time ago. I'm so sorry, my love." He whispered, looking for the floor in shame as he started crying.

"My older brother is the father to my younger brother? That is so confusing." Mingrui softly said, making Yuan sigh.

"That's the way of the Palace, unfortunately. One will get used to it the more you live here." He explained, making the younger nod as he began to understand the ways of the life he'd been born into.

"May we speak, alone that is?" Yixing asked, looking to me for an answer.

"Your Majesty, may you take the children out of the room?" I asked, looking to the other prince.

He nodded and grabbed his brother and nephew, leaving the room to Yixing and I. I held my breath as he stepped closer to me, holding a gentle smile upon his lips as he looked at me.

- Yuan pov -

I watched as the two boys happily played with one another, smiling and wishing for children to do that as well.

"Why are you staring like that?" I looked down and saw my nephew staring up at me with eyes of wonder, my brother standing beside him with an exhausted smile.

"I would like you two to be friends with your relatives as well. Treat them well and okay with them after your studies." I told them, earning nods from the two of them as I let out a gasp as I looked to the younger with a sense of realization. "You are the eldest son of the Crown Prince, which means you are next in line for the throne!"

"What?" Both of them asked, dropping their sticks and leaving their mouths wide open.

"I, I am going to be a king one day?" Shuyang asked, earning a nod from me as his brother smiled.

"That sounds like a dream!" Mingrui replied, hugging his brother with joy.

My eyes turned from the children to my brother as he came out of the residence, looking a bit disheveled but nonetheless happy as he walked over to us.

"I will talk to father. I would like my wife from long ago to be mine again." He stated, smiling at me as he planned out his wishes to greet father with.

"Did you have a pleasant conversation?" I asked, putting my thoughts together as he fixed his shirt, hiding a mark upon his neck. "The two of you were together alone for a long time."

"I will go to Father tomorrow. The sun is setting, and Huali wanted to see me today." He answered, ignoring my question as he walked away with a sense of happiness I hadn't seen in a long time.

"Who is Huali?" I stuttered as I looked to Mingrui, his big eyes full of wonder.

"She's, she's the Crown Princess, your sister in law." I softly replied, looking to Riyang's residence with concern. "I hope she knows what she's getting into if she plans to go down that route."

After sending the boys to their rooms I laid down and sighed as I heard the door open, done with talkative and inquisitive children for today. I smiled when I saw it was not a child, but someone I had affection for.

"Lin Lin, how are you tonight? I didn't expect a visit." I asked as she approached me, bowing before sitting next to my bed.

"I miss you, Your Highness, as do your children. It's been a while since you've seen them." She softly said, looking to me with a shy expression. "May I pose a question upon you, my Lord?"

"Speak, my love. You have my attention." I replied, playing with her hair as she blushed.

"Would you be delighted if you had another child, or is it frustrating for you to have three daughters?" She quietly asked, looking away as her blush became more apparent.

"Are you asking this because you're with child?" I replied making her give me a shy nod as I chuckled.

"What does that mean?" We both jumped and turned to see Mingrui standing sleepily in the corner of the room, just by the door with a confused look upon his face.

"Who are you to come into the Prince's chamber unannounced?" Lin Lin questioned, becoming agitated. I felt out a small chuckle, knowing what was to come.

5

Riyang pov -

I smiled every day as I walked past the Crown Prince and his servants. He would return the smile and slip a note for me to read later that night.

These few weeks since we moved into the palace were confusing times, with my children being removed from my hands and given to the princes to raise as their own. I'd been given freedom and a good rank, the one I was to originally have if my clan didn't abandon me, if not higher since I was in the palace.

Yixing would visit as often as he could, and we would talk all night long, or something a bit more scandal like. He promised to marry me, but his father was giving him a hard time. Despite that, he assured me that I would be his and often dropped off gifts to make my life a bit more luxurious.

But life wasn't very easy. As soon as the other princesses caught wind of who I was, they had their eyes on killing me. Not only was I the mother to a Prince of higher rank than their children, but I was also the one Yixing had his eyes on. His wife despised that my son would be the one on the throne when her son was born in the Palace rather than on the streets as Shuyang was.

"He doesn't deserve anything that has been given to him. My son deserves the throne." She hissed, slapping me across the face. I stood my ground and refused to cry, knowing it would only fuel her more.

"Shuyang didn't ask to be born by the Crown Prince, and I did not ask to become a consort for the crown." I softly said, looking to her with a smile. "I was forced into this just as much as you were, my dear Huali. Please do not disgrace my household because of your own pride being damaged."

She huffed and walked away, presumably to either Yixing or his father to request my head on a platter. Neither would give in though, since they both enjoyed my company.

"Mother, they want to change my name." I looked down to see Mingrui standing in the doorway with a pout.

"That would be reasonable since you are from the Zhang clan, not from the Fang clan," I replied, making him groan as he came to cuddle with me.

"But they don't want me to have any name from you. I will no longer be Fang Mingrui. They want me to be Zhang Rui." He whined.

"And it is a different character, I presume?" I asked, earning a nod. "Is that why you're upset, love? It's a different meaning from the one I picked for you?"

"I know it's almost the same, but it's different and it's as if they are taking me away from you. They have me living with Yuan ge's wife and children as if I'm one of them! It's frustrating." He explained, leaning on my shoulder as he pouted.

- Huali pov -

I seethed as Yixing as he came into the room, offering a curt smile as he sat down across from me.

"You requested my presence?" He asked, making me huff.

"You're touching that dirty woman, aren't you?" I questioned, making him chuckle.

"What is it to you? You know our marriage is purely political. There is no love between us." He replied, earning a laugh from me as I turned away from him.

"It took me three years to get you to look at me with anything other than contempt. It took another two until I was allowed to have a child with you. It was a blessing to have a son since he would be able to carry the throne in our name." I said, pretending to hold back tears as I glared at him. "And yet as soon as she was brought to the palace you've seen her every night."

"I love our son, but you know of my story. I loved her so much, and Father wouldn't allow me to marry her. This time, I can at least see her and be happy, even if I can't claim her as my own because you already took that position a long time ago." He replied, not even looking up to meet my gaze while he ate the meal before us.

"Would it be better for me to die? Shall I kill our son as well?" I asked, making him stop his movement and put his tools down.

"Why are you always so dramatic and demanding of me? I told you I disliked your tongue, why must you still speak so condescending towards me?" He answered, making me angry.

"I want my son on the throne, and I will do what it takes to make that happen. Do not underestimate my power in this palace." I threatened, smiling as he finally looked up at me.

"Do not underestimate my power to kill you for even threatening me." He said, scoffing at my loss of words. "Did you forget who you were married to? I am the Crown Prince. I can kill or marry whom I please, but luckily I'm a very nice person. Don't make me change that."

With that he left, and I was alone once again. I sighed, trying to calm myself down as his words left a mark upon my heart. I needed to get rid of that woman, and her mutt of a son. With a chuckle, I decided to visit my sister, Linlin. I knew she would help me since she could fall in the same predicament as I had found myself in.

"Jiejie, don't you want to keep your husband to yourself?" I asked, making her sigh as she put down her glass and rubbed her stomach absentmindedly.

"I know I have his love and affection. He only looks at me, and never even glances at anyone else." She softly said, smiling to herself.

"But what if that woman catches his eye? The two of them have been meeting for a while now. What if she produced a son?" I questioned, making her take her time looking for an answer. I smiled, knowing I had gotten under her skin.

6

Riyang pov -

"I will not allow you to marry. It doesn't matter that your son is his blood. You cannot marry him." I fell to the floor at his words, knowing I couldn't fight it without death following. "Your son will be next in line, yes, but you cannot marry him."

"Is it because I do not come from a clan?" I softly asked, not even looking up to face his wrath.

"But, your Majesty, she is my first wife. You made me lie down with her all those years ago. I fell in love with her, and yet you won't allow me to be with her?" I turned to Yixing with a look of shock, not realizing our love was bound together by us both being forced to be together.

"She is unclean. An unclean woman cannot marry a king, even if he is just a prince right now." He explained, making me start to cry.

"Your Majesty, please grant me this wish," Yixing asked, getting on his knees and bowing to his father.

"I will allow her to reside in the palace. She will not marry you, but I will grant your wish of her marrying a prince." We both looked up in confusion as a door opened, Yuan walking in with a face of disinterest. "Riyang, you shall marry my son, Yuan. Yixing is off limits because he is next in line, but I will allow you to marry into my family if that's what you wish."

"Your majesty, forgive me, but I would like to marry Yixing, not because of his status, but because of his heart." I softly said, making him chuckle.

"I understand your wishes, but life in the palace comes with a cost. Do you wish to live with peace under Yuan's house, or be killed instantly for disobedience to the emperor?" He replied, making me stutter a bit as Yuan bowed next to me.

"Just go along with it, for your son's sakes." He softly whispered, his tone telling me he didn't care for it either.

When I gave in, I was sent to my residence to prepare for the wedding. I disliked the arrangement with all my heart, but I knew I had to protect my children and make sure they live to be strong and wise.

"Mama, you're very pretty in the wedding gown." I looked to my side and smiled at Shuyang, who was giving me a gift. I held my hands open and he placed a cherry blossom in my palms. "I wanted to give you this because it reminded me of you."

"Thank you, my son. You're very thoughtful. Please stay like this, even if I can no longer see you as often as we wish." I softly replied, brushing his hair from his face and smiling.

- Yuan pov -

I walked into the residence she was now to reside in, examining the walls and sighing, trying to look everywhere except for where she was, dressed in red and waiting for my presence. Her smile was just as uncomfortable as my own was as I sat next to her.

"I know this is very uncomfortable and inconvenient for both of us, but I hope you know I will cherish you as well as I can despite my heart not being in it." I softly said, nervously playing with my sleeves.

"Are you renaming my children to fit into your family?" She asked, looking to me with innocent eyes.

"No. Father insisted on changing their names to fit our family. I dislike it as much as they do, but it would make sense since they're children of the Palace." I answered, making her nod and sigh. I glanced down as she subconsciously rubbed her hand across her stomach. "How far along are you?"

"What are you talking about?" She asked with a laugh, making me sigh and push her into the bed.

"We should make it look like the child is mine, at least for the servant's listening to us right now. Don't worry, I'll raise it as my own, though I know it is my brother's." I told her, making her shake with fear as I towered over her, gently asserting my dominance as I stripped her of her dress. I smiled when I saw her stomach already swollen with child.

"You, how did you know?" I chuckled at her shyness as I rubbed her stomach.

"My wife and I have three daughters and another child on the way. I've learned to see the pregnancy in a woman despite the layers of clothing in an attempt to hide it." I replied, giving her a small kiss on her forehead as I put her dress back to its original position, leaving her in the bed as I sat instead on the small seat. "You look about the same as my wife does, so I'd say you have four or five more months before the child is born. I'll say it was mine from before our marriage was officiated."

"Thank you, my Lord. I know I could be killed for having a child with the Crown Prince though I am a lowly consort." She softly said, sitting up and holding her arms across herself, presumably feeling embarrassed about having been exposed in front of me.

"You're very innocent for your previous job. It's adorable." I told her, making her blush. I chuckled before giving a soft bow and leaving, returning to my own chambers, where I was met with my beloved wife.

"Finished already? Was she that enjoyable that you had to leave right away?" I looked to her in confusion, her normally humble self replaced with a jealous soul as she folded her arms in irritation.

"My love, what has gotten into you? You know I would only ever want to touch you. We merely talked and drank some tea." I responded, making her laugh.

"The servants heard your sounds of pleasure and soft whispers, don't bother lying to me." She snapped, pushing a vase off the table. "I will have your children. She is nothing to you. I want my child on the throne, even if it means killing all of hers."

7

I shook in the corner of the dark room, trying to not make a sound as the woman threw the expensive goods everywhere, screaming with jealousy as my brother came back from visiting my mother.

I knew she hated me, as well as who I was born from, but I didn't think she'd want to kill me just because she hadn't born a son yet, and mother had been blessed with two sons.

"Where's that bastard child now? I'll have his head!" She screamed, throwing a vase into the corner where I was hiding. I let out a cry of pain as the piece cut up my hands as it shattered and exploded. Yuan looked over and instantly held me behind his back as his wife lurched forward to strike again.

"I don't know what has gotten into you, Lin Lin, but I will not tolerate it. If you do not stop, I will have you sent to the North Palace." He warned, making her freeze with her hand midair.

"You wouldn't dare send the mother of your children to that place." She seethed, glaring at me with death in her eyes. "Why are you protecting him? It's not as if you share a mother. There is no point in keeping him alive."

"Gege, please save me," I whispered, earning his pitiful stare as I started sobbing, the blood dripping down my hands onto the floor.

"Guards, please remove this woman from my residence. Make sure she stays alone in hers until I call her." I let out a breath of relief at his words, falling to my knees as the woman left.

He didn't say anything as he cleaned my wounds. It was just us and the sound of the wind outside, a storm rolling in from the Northern mountains. I hoped Shuyang would be alright since he'd always feared the thunder.

"Gege, I'm worried for you and Shuyang." I softly said, earning his soft eyes looking at me with concern. "You seem to be conflicted with your wife, and Xiaoyang is scared of the storms."

"Don't worry about me, Xiaorui. I will be alright. Now that you're all fixed up, why don't we go see your little brother? I'm sure he'd like to know you are concerned about his health." I smiled as he led me out of the building and down the path to my brother's residence.

- Shuyang pov -

I flinched in fear as thunder struck outside, wishing my mother or brother were here to comfort me. After I was made known to my father, he took me and had me live in his residence with him and his other children.

"Gege!" I ran to my brother and wrapped my arms around his waist, sobbing into his chest as I felt the relief of no longer being alone.

"He was worried about you, so I brought him over." I looked up and saw Yuan smiling gently down at the two of us as if fondly remembering something from his youth.

"Thank you, uncle." He chuckled at my words, still getting used to the term as I was. "Is, is my mother happy?"

"Yes. She would be happier if she got her way, but she is doing just fine. She wants you to focus on your studies and become a great prince. Treat your siblings well and your father with respect." I smiled at his words, feeling as if that's the words I needed to keep going.

I would be fine as long as she was happy. I could endure the pain my step-mother inflicted upon me. The storm would fade, as would the wounds of the past.

"Gege what happened to your hands?" I asked, noticing Mingrui's hands bandaged and bloody.

"Nothing I can't handle. But how are you doing? I noticed a limp in your step yesterday." He replied, making Yuan look at me with concern as I whimpered.

"Hua, Huali hit me. She wants her son on the throne, and dislikes me suddenly appearing and getting in her way." I softly whispered, earning a sigh from the eldest.

"That's why Lin Lin was acting up as well, or so it appears. Huali must have said something to get her so upset about you two living here now." He muttered, deep in thought as he folding his hand into a fist. "That woman has too much power in this household. I must talk to brother about this."

"Father is already dealing with it. They were talking about sending her to the northern palace as a form of exile until she recovers from her insanity." I quietly said, making him nod in agreement.

"Good. I'll still inform him of your wounds. It will push him to move up the time of departure if he hears the next in line has been beaten." He announced, smiling softly before walking away to go find my father.

Mingrui hugged me as my tears began to slip from my face. I wiped the salty water from my face as best as I could, trying to remain firm and brave despite being weak from both fear and physical pain.

"Xiaoyang, you'll be fine. It'll take some time, but we'll all be okay and become handsome and strong just as mother wants." He softly said, parting my shoulder as he tried his best to comfort me and help me recover myself.

After the thunder stopped, I bid my brother a good night and went over to my bed, tucking myself in and staring out the window. I folded my hands and closed my eyes, saying a quick prayer for strength to overcome the trials the future will bring and for health for my family, both the ones I knew a long time and those who I had just recently met.

I wished I'd listened to mother about staying in the house and not disappearing into the palace to free her. Despite my thoughts, I knew this life would be better for everyone, even if there was a struggle at this moment. I would make sure it was a better life.

8

F our Years Later

- Riyang pov -

I smiled at the sleeping child, looking at her with joy as my husband held my waist in affection.

"Feifei resembles you well, darling." He whispered, kissing my cheek and bending down to softly brush her hair from her face, gently waking her up.

"Baba." She softly said, smiling and hugging him. I chuckled, enjoying seeing their relationship strong despite the lie it was created with.

"She resembles Your Majesty as well," I replied, making him chuckle as well, our small secret hidden between ourselves. "Her brothers would like to make a visit later today if that is alright with you."

"Feifei should meet Xiaorui and Xiaofu now, they are blood after all." He replied, giving me a soft smile, knowing I disliked their new names.

"Your Majesty, Prince Rui and Prince Fu have arrived." A servant announced, earning another chuckle from Yuan as he nodded to allow them in.

"Telling them yes before I said so?" I nodded and gave him a sly smile as the boys came in, giving us both respectful bows before smiling excitedly at the small child innocently running towards them.

"Hello sister! What is your name?" Xiaofu said, smiling happily and bending down to greet his sister with a hug.

Xiaorui simply looked down before coming over to us, bowing again as he met us.

"Mother, Gege. I send greetings from the southern borders of the Palace. They have been training me well and I will not disappoint you in my combat skills when they are needed." He coldly said, looking to the floor the whole time. It made my heart break, seeing how damaged he'd become after Lin Lin tried to kill him two years ago.

When it came to light that it wasn't the first time, she was immediately sent up north alongside Huali as punishment. I felt so hurt that I couldn't help him, and when I could finally see him, he rejected my visit and left to train as a soldier.

I was happy that Xiaofu still visited me daily, after his studies and dinner with his grandfather to discuss the throne, and would stay until he was too tired to remain any longer. Both boys were growing fast, as was their sister.

"Mother, you've been going away often now. Are you feeling alright?" I looked to see Xiaofu staring at me with concern as Feifei played with her doll, no longer interested in the young man.

"I'm fine. Just somewhat tired these days." I replied, giving him a smile.

- (Ming) Rui pov -

It hurt that she ignored my words, even though I knew it was not on purpose. She wrote letters to me frequently, often asking how I was doing and telling me how much she missed me. I watched in confusion as her handwriting worsened each letter, her hands shaky and easily work out.

Now that I was seeing her, I could tell something was wrong with her. Her skin was pale, her eyes bloodshot and lips blue. She was hiding it with layers of makeup, but I could see it. I questioned how long she'd felt like this, and why she hadn't told anyone about it.

Even with my own thoughts, I couldn't open my mouth to ask her. We'd spent the last four years not speaking, me frightened with abuse and mother busy with a newborn child. She looked happy, despite her tiredness. I would not ruin that for her, no matter how curious I was about her health.

I watched as my younger brother played with our sister, happily and innocently as if he was never hurt. I wished I could do that as well, but I was scarred now. Physically, there were few wounds still showing, but internally, there were many wounds that could not be healed no matter how much time had passed.

I looked to my elder brother, examining how he looked at my mother with affection despite her tiredness and heart still taken by the Crown Prince. I could see she loved him, but not in the way he had grown in his feelings for her. I hoped she would love him the same way before her time came, which looked to be soon.

After we'd busted for a while, Shuyang and I departed, leaving after wishing the three of them health and peace. We walked in silence for a little while, trying to find our comfort like we once had. It'd been so long since we'd last seen each other, it was no longer the same as it had once been.

"Ge, I, I don't know how to talk to you anymore. We haven't seen each other in three years. We've both grown in very different ways, and I miss the way we used to be." He said, almost crying as he looked to me. I let out a sigh as he almost read my thoughts.

"It wasn't our fault we were separated. I'm sorry I haven't been there for you as of late." I replied, looking to the ground as I tried to arrange my next thought. "I, I promise I'll be by your side when you're time on the throne comes. I'll guard you until I die."

"Is that why you're training as a soldier? To be my guard once I'm king?" He asked, almost with a tearful laugh as he looked to the sky. "I know you have good intentions, but you're hurting my heart by not being by my side as we always had been."

"I'm sorry I fled. I just, I just needed to get away from all the pain that woman had put me through. Everything I saw reminded me of her, and so I needed a fresh start, even if it meant leaving you behind." I explained, looking to him for a moment. "I'm really, really sorry for abandoning you that night. I, I made your fear of thunder worse, didn't I?"

"I wish you could've just stayed away. I would have been fine if you hadn't come back." He said, glaring at me with pain in his eyes as a tear slipped from his eye.

9

I coughed as my lungs hurt, every inch of my body in pain as I lurched forward, choking on myself and spitting up blood. I had told my servants to not tell my husband, for I wanted him to live happily without knowing I was ill, but I could tell by their faces they wanted to scream it out and cry to their master about my illness.

"Mama, are you feeling better?" I turned to see Feifei looking at me with her big, wondering eyes full of concern. I smiled weakly and brushed her hair back from her face.

"I'll be alright. Don't worry about me, my love. Go find your brothers and ask for a lesson in the arts today, okay?" I softly said, coughing again into the bucket provided for my needs.

"Your Highness, His Majesty has arrived." A servant announced, making me shuffle as I tried to hide my sickness as he came through the door.

"Yuan, I'm not feeling good today. I haven't even out on my make up yet." I said, covering my face as I tried to hide the blood still dripping from my mouth.

"Riyang, I know you've been sick for some time. Why can't you tell me what is happening so that I can see if I can help you?" He softly asked, hugging me as he revealed my lips to his sight.

"I'm fine." I replied just as I start coughing again.

"It's poison, isn't it?" He asked, earning a fearful pout from me as he guessed his answer. "Are you doing this to yourself?"

"I wouldn't purposefully drink poison, even if I disliked my living situation. I, I have affection for you as if you were my own blood, and I wouldn't want to leave my children behind in such a cruel manner." I explained, looking down in shame. "But they've been serving me this tea for years now. There's no point in trying to fix it when I know it's too late."

"Who? I will take care of them." He questioned, looking as is he was trying to calm his anger. I lightly out my hand upon his chest, bracing myself on him as my legs wanted to do anything but support my stance.

"It's no use. She's already exiled. But she has servants who are loyal to her despite her no longer being in the palace." I answered, making him tighten his fists.

"Huali or Lin Lin?" He asked, earning a chuckle.

"I want to see Yixing. I, I don't know how much longer I have for this world. I'm sorry, Yuan, but can you please fetch him for me?" I answered, changing the subject as I sat down, no longer able to stand up. He kneeled in front of me, looking at me with pain in his eyes.

"Can't I be the one you love?" He begged, showing his fragility as he started to cry, the first time before me in a long time. He took my hand and placed it upon his lips, giving it a tender kiss. "Please, can't I have your heart this time?"

- Yixing pov -

I walked down the hall with a nervous heart. Yuan's servant said it was important that I visit Riyang today, and it made me fearful of what would happen. Did Yuan finally get mad at her not loving him? Did something happen to Feifei? These thoughts ran through my mind as I quickly traveled to her residence.

"You've arrived?" Yuan stated, smiling sadly at me as he greeted me at the door. I mirrored the smile as I greeted him in return.

"What is the matter that I must pause my royal duties as King to see you and your wife, my dear brother?" I asked, both knowing I'd rather do anything with Riyang than do what I was born for as Crown Prince.

"She, she didn't tell you either?" He returned the question, making my heart waver more so as his voice broke.

"What's wrong with Riyang?" I asked, walking past him to see her weakly smiling from her bed, looking as if death had his strong grip on her. "Riyang, what's the matter?"

"She's been drinking poisoned tea for at least three years now. Whatever is was, it's strong enough to kill her this quickly rather than the several years it would take according to the medical books." Yuan explained, looking heartless as he turned towards his wife, my one and only love. "This fool didn't tell a soul what was going on."

"But, why? Riyang why would you drink it?" I looked to her for an answer. She smiled and stretched out her hand, beging for mine to be placed within it's grasp.

I looked to Yuan for permission, before taking her hand in my own. I felt her coldness and weak pulse, and knew she was barely clinging on to life.

It made my heart clench, knowing I could've stopped it if she had told me when it first began.

"I need to tell you something. It's a very serious and important matter I've been hiding for a few years now." She softly said, looking to Yuan with a saddened expression as she took a breath.

"I give you permission to reveal your secrets, my love." He quietly replied, making me heart wrench again for her as she started coughing again.

"What is it that you need to tell me? Can't we just sit here and hold each other for a while?" I asked, making her smile, weakly chuckling as she gripped my hand a little tighter.

"It is a very important matter that you must know of. My heart will not rest in peace unless you know the truth of this matter." She whispered, eyes closing for a second as she tried to organise her thoughts as best as she could.

"My love, should I tell him? You should rest now. We'll be here with you the entire time you need us." Yuan asked, earning a shake of her head.

"I need to do it." She looked back to me with a heartbroken smile as she wheezed a bit more. "Yixing, I need to tell you. Feifei, my little angel, she is your daughter."

10

- -

S ix Years Later

- Fu (Shuyang) pov -

I placed my hands roughly upon my brother, glaring up at him as he remained stoic and firm in his stance. I shoved him into the wall and started crying, punching his chest, praying he would show emotions as his siblings were being attacked by others.

"Rui ge, please. Can't you see Xiaofei and I are suffering at the hands of Huali and Lin Lin?" I asked, looking up into his eyes with my tears flowing. "You promised you'd protect me."

"You told me you never wanted to see me again, since I made you the victim to a monster the moment I left. I'm merely keeping your wishes." He replied, looking back with an almost dead expression.

"Ge, you know I was just upset because mother was ill. You know I didn't mean those words, so why are you so mean to me now?" I asked, brushing off my Hanfu and turning away from my elder. "Even if you aren't going to protect me, at least protect your sister. She needs you more than I do."

With those final words, I left him in the library, no longer wanting anything to do with him. I made my way to the throne room, smiling as I was met with my father. After bowing, I walked over and sat in my seat beside his.

"Father, you must realize what the queen is doing to your son. I hope you will deal with it accordingly." I harshly said, looking down as my irritation began to show again.

"She will be dealt with. She killed your mother, and is now trying to get rid of you as well. She still wishes for her son to have the throne." He replied, sighing as he out down his scrolls.

"I know my little brother did nothing wrong, nor does he wish for the throne. Please be merciful on him, father." I asked, making him chuckle as he let my hair.

I could see in his eyes he was still missing mother, though she had long since left this world. I couldn't deny that he saw my pain as well, since I was closest to her and was there when she was buried. We sat in silence for a moment, lost in our memories as we let go of our pain. I knew that, one day, we would get past this pain and become stronger.

- Yuan pov -

"Feifei I'm going to visit the western borders today. I won't return for a few weeks. Will you be alright while I am away?" I asked, looking down to the small girl who was sewing an elaborate design onto a ribbon.

"Yes father. I will await your return as always. Fu ge treats me well, and I know he will protect me from Her Majesty if she makes a move against us while you are visiting the border." She replied, looking up with a smile.

It made me smile with pride, seeing how mature she was for being so young. I knew Yixing ge and I were quite reckless at her age, as were her brothers. I pet her hair before leaving, wishing my other daughters well as

I made my way to the carriage that would carry me to the place far away from the palace.

The view was pretty, the roads quite exquisitely pleasing as I travelled. The days were taking longer than I wanted, as the snow began to fall by the time I reached the one residence I'd been looking forward to seeing for the past six months. I saw the figure I knew so well standing underneath a cherry blossom tree, the last flowers falling into her grasp as she smiled, hair flowing freely now that she was free.

"Yuan." I pressed my lips against hers the moment she said my name, making her gasp in surprise, but return the gesture nonetheless.

I led her inside and kissed her again, making her blush as I pushed her against the wall and continued pressing my lips to hers.

"Yuan, please. Your servants are still outside. They will be able to hear us if we continue like this." She softly begged, though her eyes told me to continue.

"Alright, but I missed you so much I am just having a hard time constraining my urges to kiss you until you are too weak to resist my charms." I replied, making her chuckle as her face became the same color as her dress.

"You don't have to kiss me to make me surrender to your charms. Just tell the servants to leave for the evening and return in the morning. I'm sure they would like to stay somewhere warm as the evening is coming, and more snow will surely fall." She explained, earning a red tint from my own cheeks as my excitement got the better of me.

I quickly told the servants that they should return in two days time, since I had lots of business to discuss with the woman residing here, earning knowing looks from them all. They all silently obeyed, bowing and taking their things, departing and leaving me to myself and my lover.

When I returned, her hair was let down a little more, and she had a flirtatious smile upon her lips as she waited for me on her bed.

"Are you so needy as to tell them to leave for so long?" She asked, making me chuckle as I laid down beside her, my hand tracing her hair with seductive eyes.

"My love, you're just as needy to already be in your sleepwear, knowing it is much, much easier to remove that simple article of clothing off of your beautiful body." I replied, inching a little further in as she smirked and turned away out of embarrassment. She shivered as I placed my lips upon her neck, making her weak and malleable to my will.

"Yuan, I am yours to take control of, no need to be so slow about it." She whispered, earning a chuckle from me as I kissed her upon her sweet lips.

"I love you, Riyang."

11

I collapsed after I'd spoken those words to Yixing, my eyes closing as my heart gave out. When I woke up, I assumed I'd made my way into either heaven or the afterlife by the way everything was so soft and bright.

"My love, you're awake." I turned and saw Yuan sitting beside my head, his hand gently holding mine as he looked at me with worry. "The doctors said that they might not be able to save you, but I didn't want to give up."

"Where, where am I?" I questioned, taking in a deep breath for the first time in what felt like a long time.

"Far away from the palace. We even held a memorial service in your name." He explained, making me look at him in confusion. "Fang Riyang is now dead, according to the public files. You are living in Jiayuguan, a good sixteen days travel from the capital, and you are residing under the name Lu Meihua."

"Why, why did you save me? Why couldn't I just die?" I asked, letting out a sob as I regained my memory.

"Because you are my wife. I will not let you go until I am ready to die. We shall die together, my love when we are fat and old and have plenty of grandchildren to spoil." He replied, earning my glance. He truly meant his words, and it hurt my heart to see him with so much honesty when I knew my heart belonged to his brother.

"You'll, you'll help me love you the way you love me?" I softly asked, making him smile and nod, happy that I was finally giving him a chance.

The way his lips curled into that smile made me want to love him. He deserved it, after all these years of ignoring him while he fell for me was harsh. I needed to repay him with my heart and soul.

The years passed and I fell in love with him. He never spoke of the past, and only focused on my health and happiness. We ended up having a son together, naming him Zhennan, and raising him with the best happiness a boy could receive.

I still thought of the past I had left behind, my sons and my little girl. It was hard to try to forget them, especially when Yuan still lived with them and continued to raise Feifei on his own, as I was doing with Zhennan. He told me not to worry, for they all have forgotten my existence.

All I wished for was to see my children be together once more.

Yixing POV

I received news that my brother was visiting someone outside of the Palace, sometimes for days at a time. This made me suspicious of him, and I prayed he was not planning a rebellion. I didn't care if it was a Mistress, though I would prefer he stay inside the palace walls for his own safety.

I decided to question him in it, but I saw he was already leaving before I could walk up to him. I glanced at my youngest brother, Xiaorui, and he nodded, silently accepting my quiet request.

I prayed for his safety as he hopped on his horse and fled, chasing after the carriage carrying our brother.

"Father, why does it concern you that he meets someone out of the palace?" I turned to see Xiaofu staring at me with a confused expression. I smiled and greeted him happily.

"Because, my son, if he is meeting with a man, it is to revolt, and it could mean our lives. And if he is meeting with a woman, it means he wants to hide her. This is suspicious since all women of the palace should reside in its walls." I explained, earning a nod of understanding.

"So we must wait on my brother's report." He replied solemnly, turning, and walking back towards his palace to greet his bride.

"Zongying, greetings my child," I said as she bowed respectfully to the two of us.

"Greetings to Your Highness, Your Majesty. I have come to inform you of the news you have been waiting for." She softly said, earning smiles from both Xiaofu and I.

"You are with child?" Xiaofu asked excitedly, sanding a nod and a smile from the girl as she started shaking, tears falling from her face as her husband embraced her.

"Let's pray it is a son so that you can carry the throne in my place when I get too old to do so," I told them, earning a bow from both of them before they left to go celebrate on their own.

I walked back to my palace, finding myself thinking about the love that had left me behind to join the stars above. I hoped she was alright up there, and enjoying herself as she waited for me to join her in the afterlife.

I let myself shed a tear, knowing she would be overjoyed to have a grand-child on the way, just as she was happy to see her sons grow into handsome and capable young men.

The days passed and I got more anxious as Xiaorui didn't return as quickly as I had expected him to do. I wondered if Yuan had discovered his presence and killed him, or if the winter snow had caught up to him and made it impossible to survive the night.

Just as a heavy storm lay waste to the grounds outside the palace, a door slammed open. I looked up to see a shivering Xiaorui running in, collapsing in front of me with fear in his eyes.

"What happened?" I asked, helping him up and to the fireplace. He panted, tired, and cold as the snow worsened.

"Ge, she, she's still alive." He whispered, earning a worrisome expression from me, as I could barely understand him with his shaking.

"What do you mean? Who's, who's still alive?" I questioned, making him turn to me with fear and pain written in his eyes.

"My mother."

12

X iao Rui's POV

I kept my horse quiet as we trotted closer to the building that Yuan ge went into. After he dismissed his servants, I could hear the sounds of laughter and lovemaking, which made me almost vomit. Though pleasurable to most people, I found those sounds to be of something I never wanted.

Shaking my head to ignore my own thoughts, I tied my horse to the nearest tree and continued to sneak closer alone. I made it inside the house, but I stopped when I heard a creak behind me.

"Who are you?" I turn around and see a child, no more than five years old, sleepily staring at me.

"I, I work for the man in this room. I just need to tell him something." I quickly replied, making him tilt his head in confusion.

"Baba doesn't allow anyone in here when he's talking to Mama." The child explained, making me falter in my step.

"He's, he's your father?" I asked, earning a small nod. I let out a breath of frustration and opened the door to the room Yuan and his lover were in.

It was almost slow motion, the shock of my surprise awakening. I saw him flinch away, and I saw her eyes, the ones I grew up next to, look upon me with fear. He covered her, but it was too late, for I had already seen who it was.

My heart shattered, and I fled. I heard her calling after me, but I ignored it, getting on my horse and riding as far away as I could.

"It had to be a ghost," I whispered, crying as the horse sped down the forest trail. "It's impossible for him to have saved her."

I was still a few miles from the palace when my horse fell, screaming as it's leg snapped. I flew off of the saddle, wincing as my own limbs suddenly shot pain through my body. Ignoring my own pain, I drew my sword and ended the creature's pain, grabbing my bag off of its corpse and continuing to run home.

The snow began to come down harshly, but I couldn't just stop and lay down. I knew if I did that, I would only begin crying.

If it was just my imagination, I would be fine and be able to move on. If it wasn't, my heart wouldn't be able to take it. It would be as if she left us just to be free. A betrayal, something I just couldn't handle.

I fled to the only house I could seek comfort in, my brother opening the door immediately as I stumbled in, cold and broken.

Yuan POV

I ran after Xiao Rui as fast as possible, but I couldn't stop him as he stumbled out of the residence and fled to his horse. I returned inside and saw Zhennan sleepily staring at me with his mother holding him.

"What are we going to do?" She asked, her nerves getting the better of her. I kissed her forehead gently and took the tired child from her arms.

"We will discuss this in the morning. Rest will clear our minds." I softly answered, walking to put our son in his bed.

I retired to our room, laying down beside her as she shivered with fear. I kissed her gently, reminding her that I took her away from the palace, and I would never let her be dragged back in.

"I will return to talk with my brother. You and the child shall stay here." I told Riyang as the three of us ate breakfast. She nodded with understanding, the boy just eating since he didn't have the knowledge of his mother's past or my position.

When I got back to the palace, I went straight to Xiao Rui's residence, slamming his door and pushing him against a wall.

"Do you not know what you have done?" I asked, glaring at him as he stared blankly.

"I did my job for my king and my country. What you have done is a betrayal to the throne." He answered, earning a slap from me, which made him laugh. "I spent this entire time in the military, do you think a slap will scare me?"

"Would you like me to slit your throat?" I growled, pulling out a blade and placing it against his pale skin. He didn't even flinch, merely chuckling again.

"Would your wife be happy if you killed her son?" I faltered, letting him get the higher ground as he whipped his hands so fast I couldn't even process his actions as he flipped us over and held the knife to my own throat. "Or would she be sad that her son killed his brother?"

"Neither of you are going to die, for today at least." I looked past the young man threatening my life to see my older brother and his eldest son standing in the doorway, glares etched in both of their faces.

"Ge, what do you want? This is a matter between the two of us." I stated, smiling and laughing as they didn't budge.

"We know what Rui ge saw. He reported it immediately to the king. You must explain yourself, or face the consequences of rebelling against the crown." Xiaofu stated. I would almost be proud of how he grew up and how his speech had shown great improvement if he wasn't threatening my life.

"You will come to the court in an hour, I will give you time to clean yourself up," Yixing commanded, pulling his son and our brother out of the room.

I watched as a guard remained with me, a cold glare set upon his face. He remained by my side, not once leaving, even as I made my way to the court that would decide my fate. I wondered whether I should lie or if I should beg for his forgiveness and give in to whatever he desires me to do.

Only time would tell what I would end up deciding to do.

13

I glared at the man standing before me. If I had been innocent, he would've merely been an uncle I cared for. But I knew what he did, who he'd been hiding. Now, he was a man I wanted vengeance against for taking my life away from me.

My father held me back, his compassion and wisdom keeping me honorable before the court. I watched as my brother walked in, bowing and paying respects to both me and my father.

"Confess to your crimes. There is no point in hiding it." My father said, staring at his younger brother with a pained expression.

Yuan looked to the floor, bowing and kneeling to the ground. He began to sob, mumbling about his life being spared for the words he was about to speak.

"Please, just relate to us the words you are demanded of. We are prepared for any damaging news." I complained, earning a glare from my father and a chuckle from my brother.

"I, I was tired of my brother getting everything handed to him. The girl belonged to me, but she was given to him. He laid down with her and produced children with him, all while I desired her." He explained, chuckling as his thoughts became words. "As soon as she had given birth to the child, I began to poison her. Just enough for her to believe she was dying, but it was quite an easy cure once I took her out of the capital."

He looked to me, then to my brother, then to my father, smiling as he saw our confused expressions.

"I told her that you all had given up on her, no longer cared for the whore she is. She was finally mine, giving me all I wanted whenever I wanted it." Yuan began to laugh as he finished his thoughts, our anger showing as his humor drowned us all. "I had almost completely gotten away with it if it wasn't for this bastard son of my father."

"Don't speak of my brother like that." I hissed, earning a chuckle from him as he stood up and walked right up to Rui, slapping him with so much force he fell to the ground.

My brother didn't cry, though, instead just staring at him as if it was nothing he hadn't suffered before. Rui wiped the blood from his mouth and stood back up, returning to his original posture as if nothing had occurred.

"What is the meaning of hitting your flesh and blood?" My father asked, making Yuan chuckle again.

"He is no brother of mine. He's the son of a harlot, worth nothing to me nor the throne. Why should you care for him as if he was anything more than grass for us to tread on?" He replied, making me coil my fists in an attempt to remain calm. "Why would you turn your back on the true son of the throne in order for this whore's son to claim it?"

"You dare speak of the Crown Prince in such a manner?" Rui asked, aggressiveness in his stance as he threatened to defend me with his blood.

Xiaofei's POV

I pushed past the guards and forced my way into the court where my father and brothers were discussing the crimes and evil deeds committed by the one who raised me.

I saw my brother almost ready to slit my father's throat, the King and the Crown Prince watching in anger. They all turned in surprise when I came running in, slipping between Rui ge and my father to protect him.

"He does not deserve death! It's merely a Mistress, what is the big deal?" I shouted, making Fu ge laugh as he tried to keep his tears at bay.

"You are still innocent, little one. I see you did not know the words he just spoke to us." He told me, looking to my father. "Do tell, since she is your kin. Or, would you like us to reveal the truth to her for you?"

"Don't okay games like that with me. She is innocent on this, I will do no such thing as ruining her youth by saying anything." I turned to my father, backing up to stand next to my brothers. "Feifei, return home. You don't need to be here for this."

"Fuqin, I will not obey you today. I must know, no matter the cost." I replied, eyes glaring with curiousness as my brother gingerly held my hand.

"I would rather die than spill those words." He answered, spitting at the ground before grabbing my brother's sword and holding it against his own throat. "Would you like to have me end my own life?"

"Would your wife like to see you die?" Uncle asked, making father falter. We all turned to see where he was staring, and I fell to the ground at the sight of the ghost in the corner, crying and holding a child.

"Ri, Riyang what are you doing here?" Father stuttered, dropping the sword and walking over towards her. She backed away, holding the child close as she protected herself from him.

"Is it true? All the words you spoke?" She whimpered, making me even more confused. The ghost was so life-like, it felt surreal to see mother standing there, shaking in fear at father.

"You, you heard?" He fell to his knees and held her skirt, begging for her attention as she looked up to Uncle.

"Did you truly miss me?" Uncle nodded, no longer keeping his composure as he let his tears fall. I watched as my brothers ran to the ghost, holding her tightly.

Father dropped his hands, letting the woman come forward to greet them.

I realized she was not a ghost, that my mother was standing before me with tears in her eyes as she held my brothers in her arms. I started crying, running over to her as well.

"Ma!" I shouted, earning a smile from her.

"My little Feifei, how you have grown." She softly said, brushing my hair back.

"I will not sit back and watch all of my work fall apart." We all gasped as he grabbed the small child that mother had come in with, holding a sword to his neck. "I will kill both him and myself if you go back to this life."

14

R iyang POV

I lurched forward to grab my son, but Yuan pulled him back farther from my reach. Zhennan was crying, begging his father to stop his actions because it was scaring him.

"Yuan, stop this," I begged, getting on my knees and holding my hands as if I was praying to the gods above.

"Do you think I am not serious about going through with this?" He asked, making me sob as I looked into his eyes.

"Please, I am begging you, do not kill our child," I answered, bowing to him as low as I could go. "If, if you are to kill someone today, let it be me. My heart is not faithful to you. Zhennan is innocent, let him live."

"Should I?" He asked with a chuckle, dropping both child and sword as he came up to me, wrapping his hands around my throat. "You're a ghost already, I should just make it a reality, no?"

"Baba stop!" Feifei shouted, her brothers pulling their swords out as Yixing unsheathed his.

"Not, not in front of the children," I whispered, my airway blocked too much to allow me to think of anything but protecting the life I'd brought into the world.

"There is nothing left for me to do except kill you, I will not spare their eyes." He growled, tightening his grip.

Feifei and Zhennan screamed as their father was stabbed, Rui being quick and precise with his blade. Yuan dropped me and fell to the floor, gasping as he held his side.

"Put him in the prison," Rui said opening the door for the guards to come in. "It's not a life-threatening wound, but make sure to clean and bandage it."

I watched as Rui picked me up and carried me to the infirmary, my own son carrying me instead of I lifting him. He didn't look hurt, though I saw his lip swelling from the hit he received earlier.

"You grew up so much." I softly said, brushing his hair from his face as he set me down upon the bed, the doctor coming over immediately.

"Her neck was injured, please care for her." He said, not looking at me once.

It hurt to see him as if he was in pain at the thought of looking towards me, but I understood his pain. After we came to the palace, I hadn't been there for him, sending him away in order to care for Feifei and the palace requirements. He'd had nothing except pain and rejection the entire time he was growing up.

I knew it was my doing, and that I did nothing to rescue him, even after I had escaped that life. Now that I had returned, he no longer wanted me in his life, and I knew I had to respect that decision, no matter how badly it broke my heart to see him walk away from me with no intentions of looking towards me anymore.

Xiaorui POV

I sighed, sliding down the wall to the floor just outside the infirmary. My heart was in pain to see her again, knowing it was not an illusion that night.

"Is Mama okay?" I looked up and saw the small boy from before, looking to me with fear. I offered a soft smile and nodded.

"She'll be alright," I answered, making him nod happily and sit beside me, pulling from his pocket a small snack and offering it to me.

"Thank you for stopping Baba." He said, sighing with a saddened expression. "You, you are Uncle?"

"Yes, I'm Uncle," I replied, earning a smile from the small boy. "I am Zhang Rui."

"Will Uncle take care of me from now on?" I looked back to the boy, who was now looking up at me with tears in his eyes.

"Do, do you need me to?" I asked, gaining an enthusiastic nod from him. "Why?"

"Baba is not nice. Mama cries often. I, I don't think they will be happy anytime soon." He whispered, fiddling with his sleeves. "Can you take care of me please?"

"I promise," I replied, grabbing his hand and staring him gently in the eyes. "From now on, Uncle Rui will take care of Little Zhennan."

I let him sleep in my bed as I went to speak with Xiaofu. I looked to a maid with suspicion, not recognizing her as she walked past me towards the infirmary. Despite knowing what I had to speak to Xiaofu about was important, I decided to follow the maid.

"Did Yuan send you?" I heard my mother ask, making me freeze even when I knew I shouldn't.

"He asked me to relay the message that you can never escape him, even in death." The maid softly answered, causing my heart to start racing.

"I understand." I knew I had to move, or else it would be too late to stop what I knew was happening behind the closed door of the infirmary room before me.

I slammed the door open, causing the maid to look at me in fear as she dropped the blade she was holding, falling to the ground and bowing, asking for forgiveness. I spared her no mercy as I slit her throat with my sword, ending her life without blinking my eyes.

I looked to my mother, her eyes soft as she gasped for air, a deep wound in her abdomen that was gushing with blood. I dropped to my knees and held her hand, crying as I, again, couldn't save her as I had promised when I was young.

"I'm finally free. Don't be sad." She struggled to get her words out as she weakly squeezed my hand, smiling as she looked to the heavens.

I sobbed as her hand went limp, no longer holding mine as her ragged breathing stopped. I was hurt, saddened, and angered. With one last kiss to her hand, I grabbed my sword and ran from the room, knowing what I had to do.

15 (Final Chapter)

Xiaorui POV

I ran towards the prison, anger coursing through my veins as I held my sword in my hand. Being the Head of the Guards, I knew exactly where he was, and I laughed as I came up to his cell, opening the door and walking in to see him look at me without any emotion.

"I see my maid carried through since she is not here." He told me, chuckling as I came closer to him, my hands steady as I aimed my blade towards him. "Do it, what is stopping you?"

"Nothing, bastard," I replied, driving the weapon through his chest, making sure I hit his vital organs this time. I pushed him to the wall, digging it in as best as I could as I laughed. "You killed her. This is her vengeance. You will not see her again, even in the next life, I'll make sure of it."

When I slid my blade out, he fell to the ground, no longer a problem for anyone in this life. I fell to the floor and began crying, mourning the true loss of my mother after years of thinking she was already gone.

We held a small funeral for her, seeing she was already dead in the records. I held both Feifei and Zhennan close, my siblings losing both of their parents in a single day. Xiaofu was standing silently, trying to not cry as he held his wife, now swollen with child. He needed to act tough for her, in order to keep her safe from the chaos our family brought.

Later, after the ceremony was over, I pulled him to the side to speak with him in private.

"I wanted to talk to you before this happened, but I could not find a chance to. My apologies." I softly said, looking down in shame. "I, I know it doesn't matter anymore since your father is adopting our sister while I am taking Zhennan with me, but I wanted to let you know that I won't be coming back to the palace for a long time. I wanted you to take care of our siblings, but this is no longer necessary."

"Why, where are you going?" He asked, his gentle self holding me close as tears welled in his eyes.

"I have been assigned to be the representative of our nation. I will be traveling to Edo by the end of next month." I explained, making him whine. "I will also be making a stop in Joseon before being a permanent resident in Edo."

"Ge, that's so far away! Why did you say yes to such a mission?" He questioned, holding me closer as he let his tears fall. "Mother just died, my wife is with child, and you're leaving me alone to go across the sea?"

"I'm sorry, but I could not refuse the mission. I, I will return as soon as I can. You can keep this as a token of my promise."

Xiaofu POV

I whined as he handed me his favorite hairpiece, the cold metal contrasting with my warm skin.

"Ge, why are you leaving me?" I asked, no longer holding back my sobs.

"I want to travel the world, see how big it is. This was the only way to do so. I will be back." He explained, hugging me and petting my hair before walking away.

I cried for a small while before I returned back to my residence, Zongying ready sleeping as soundly as she could with her enlarged stomach. With a sigh, I laid down beside her and held her close, giving her a small kiss upon her hand as she moved to make more room for me.

The next day it was announced that Feifei would be married to a prince from Joseon. I gasped and looked to Rui with a knowing look, to which he simply smiled and looked away.

Zongying smiled and grabbed her sister's hand, excitedly sharing how fun it is to travel from the Palace. I walked over to my brother and folded my arms.

"Is that your 'little stop' in Joseon?" I asked, earning a nod as he chuckled. "Is that why you are so excited to go? To get rid of her?"

"No, of course not. I'm actually very sad to see her go. I'm excited because I will also be marrying someone once I get to Japan, to help boost our peaceful relations." He explained, earning a gasp from me, which made him laugh again. "Why are you so surprised? Did you think I'd die with no children?"

"No, no I just didn't expect you to want to get married. I thought you'd be one of those bachelors that would visit harems for their entire youth." I replied, earning a punch from him, causing us both to laugh.

It was one of the last times we saw each other before his departure, but it was the happiest we'd been in a long time. I knew we had forgiven any strife we may have had as children, and we grew to be strong young men with a close bond to one another.

I bid him a safe journey, congratulating both him and Feifei on their marriages, blessing them with many children and happy lives. I wanted nothing but peace for my family for the rest of our lives, knowing how much trouble we had as children.

I watched as my father aged and my children grew up, happy, and at peace with innocence and contentment with their lives at the Palace. It was a sight I didn't want to lose as I got older as well, smiling and laughing with my siblings over family meals disguised as national banquets, their own children being fluent in all the languages they'd come to know as they were raised in their own palaces so far away from where their parents were raised.

It made me rest easy, knowing we had peace and happiness at last.

The End

* Edo and Joseon are the names for Japan and Korea at the time setting for this story

* There will be an epilogue showing the lives of Feifei and Rui after leaving China

*I might make another book based off of Zhennan's POV (let me know if you're interested!)

* Thank you for reading and (hopefully) enjoying the story!

Epilogue I

Feifei's POV

I pouted as I sat in the carriage with my brothers, awaiting the long journey to meet the boy I was to marry. I was only upset at the fact that I had to leave my home, and to travel to a place so vastly different from my own was terrifying. I heard stories that they were very nice and gentle people, but I knew that in the palace was a different story.

It always was. No matter the country, there was always strife and wars within the walls of the palace the Royal Family resided in. And I was scared to have something terrible happen in a foreign land.

The only comfort I had was that my brother would be there to make sure I was alright, even if it was for a short time. I didn't have to travel alone, and that made me relax a little more.

"Princess Feifei, greetings to Your Highness." The king kindly greeted us, making me feel better as his sons came in and lined up in a row to greet their newest member. "These are my sons, you will be marrying the eighth one, Wang Eun."

"Greetings, sir." I softly said to each one of them, blushing at how handsome each of the twelve were. I smiled at the eighth, memorizing his face with a sense of peace. "Good day, My Lord."

"To you as well, Your Highness." He softly replied, his innocence making me giddy. We were to be two innocent doves with one another, and that was cute to me.

"My brother carries the gifts and the authority to my being given in marriage." I gently informed the ruler of the nation, motioning to Rui ge to give him the papers he requested.

After the wedding ceremony, I bid farewell to my brothers, who were continuing their journey to another country. I knew I would miss them, and I looked forward to seeing them again one day.

"Bibi, can you, can you teach me Mandarin?" I turned to see the one I married, smiling at his little accent upon my name. It was cute, something I liked a lot from only him. "I want, I want to say your name correctly."

"I prefer your way of saying it. It's really adorable and feels affectionate when coming from you." I replied, earning a blush from the boy. "But, if you'd like, I can teach you the language so that we can have our own little world, even when surrounded by others."

"Could we?" He asked, trying to hide his excitement. I nodded, and off we fled to our residence to go learn each other's language.

We were both children forced to become adults, so it was a shelter for us to rely on one another. We grew close very quickly, which was against my own original prejudice of him. This made me joyful, that I could call his arms my home.

Two Years Later

The boy was happy he wasn't eligible for the throne, because it meant he could spend more time with me rather than his studies, but I worried for him and his life that I held dear.

"My Lord, I fear for your safety in this palace." I softly said, holding him close as we laid together in his bed. He chuckled and brushed my hair from my face.

"Why do you have anything to worry about? I'm perfectly fine, and I won't leave for the next life until I am old." He asked, looking into my eyes with humor.

"I've read the history books of both your and my own palace. Lots of kings, when reaching the throne, would kill their brothers in order to ensure the crown stays in his own bloodline." I answered, sighing as I held his face in my hands, gently rubbing my thumbs across his jawline. "I, I'm scared for you, my dear husband."

"Hyungnim wouldn't ever think of hurting us. He loves us all, even granting us land to move to when we grow older." He explained, kissing my forehead. "If it would make you feel better, we can move there now."

I nodded and pouted, earning a chuckle from him. He softly rubbed the swollen stomach between us, making me blush as he smiled with pride.

"I will protect you both then, and we shall set off in two days' time. Does that sound good?" He asked, making me smile and kiss his cheek happily.

We didn't go to the land his brother had provided, instead hiding in a small village out near the borders of my home country. I sighed with both mourning and relief as my thoughts had come true, and the eldest boy shed the blood of his brothers in order to keep his throne.

Wang Eun held my hand tightly as I went into labor early due to the stress his brother was causing. The neighbors, fortunately, were very kind and understanding, helping us despite not knowing our full story.

"You two were blessed with a son as your first child!" The woman said, happily smiling at us as we breathed out a laugh of joy. "You were also given a daughter to share his gift of life."

"There, there were two?" I asked, earning an excited nod as her daughter came in, carrying another child wrapped in a blanket.

Seonghun and Seonghyeon were around six years old when we received news that the new king had died, and since he had no heirs, the Palace was in an uproar on who would be the next king. Since Wang Eun was the last heir to the previous king, he was in line.

"Is it okay for us to return?" He asked, holding me close and kissing me softly as we watched our children play with the villagers, not knowing their blood was royal.

"Do we have a choice? You would be the best king compared to anyone those court eunuchs would decide upon." I replied, earning a sigh and a nod from him as he couldn't help but agree.

We decided to be the change the country needed. Wang Eun took no other wife nor concubine and only kept me by his side. We were blessed to have many children, and we made sure to raise them to be the best people they could become.

My brothers were very proud of what I had accomplished without them watching me, and that made me smile as I watched them improve their own countries as well.

Fu ge made our homeland a peaceful one, with many riches and people. Rui ge helped make Edo a prosperous country, even cutting back on childhood deaths by adopting so many of the orphans left behind by those who didn't want or couldn't afford to raise the children.

The three of us united the different countries and made a strong national tie between the three regions. And we all were very happy with our work.

Epilogue II

I laughed as Feifei pouted, getting into the carriage with me as we were preparing for our journey south.

"I don't even speak their language, how am I to marry a man there?" She asked, folding her arms as she pouted again. "Stop laughing, Ge, it's not funny!"

"Do you think I understand the tongue if the people I'm traveling to? I'm just as nervous as you are." I replied, causing her to look up in surprise. "I know, me being nervous does not sound possible. But, trust me, I'm always nervous when I have to let you out of my sight, both of you."

She ruffled Zhennan's hair, causing him to whine. I let out a soft chuckle, staring at the two of them as if they actually were my children instead of my siblings.

I watched them as they slept, the long journey tiresome for their small frames. It made me smile that I could travel with them on my way to my new place of residence.

The journey for Feifei came to an end, and we all greeted the King of Joseon and the prince to marry her. Zhennan was excited to see a boy his age there as we were preparing for the wedding, making me laugh as they became best friends over the time period we are there, not even worrying about the language barrier as they both played the same games.

I gave her away to the prince, who was blushy and shy as he stuttered out his excitement in broken Mandarin. Feifei smiled and laughed, finally at peace with her new home when she repeated the words back to him in broken Korean.

After the journey over the sea, Zhennan and I arrived at the palace in Kyoto. We were greeted by the newly appointed King, who was near my age.

"Greetings. I am Hirota Ryo. You are Zhang Rui?" He asked, earning a nod and a bow from me as I bid my hellos to him.

"I see. You were supposed to marry my sister, but she, unfortunately, had a weak heart and left this world before you arrived. We couldn't get a message to you, my deepest apologies." He told me, making me laugh. "Why is this a humorous matter to you?"

"My Lord, it is because I found it funny that a message was not delivered. I was in Joseon for three months before traveling here, and even then my brother did not send a message my way." I explained, earning a laugh from him.

"I see, that is a matter worth laughing over." He replied, calming himself down. "I can still use you as a representative if you'd like to stay."

"I didn't plan on returning at any time near," I told him, earning a smile from him. "I hope we can be good friends for the time I am a resident here."

One Year Later

I let out a soft moan as he held me against the wall of his bedroom, his lips attacking my neck to the point that I couldn't breathe. His hands were masterful at stripping me of my garments, a habit we knew so well.

"Rui, I'm happy you didn't flee the first time I kissed you." He softly said, pausing to look at me with hooded eyes, the man before me already drunk on his lust as he laid me down upon his bed.

"Ryo, I thought I was alone in the world until I met you," I replied, making him chuckle as he sat up to remove his garments.

"You'll never be alone, as long as I live." He softly said, kissing me again.

Our marriage was just as fancy as Feifei's was, the splendor and the feast lighting up the rooms for all to see. Zhennan was excited to be a Prince of Japan after the marriage, making me laugh as the boy did his best to learn the ways of the land he was to be raised in as my son rather than my nephew.

I was very excited to tell my brother the news, but I decided to surprise him with it the next time we visited one another, which would most likely be at the next Imperial Banquet that Ryo and I were invited to.

The months passed and we finally traveled back to my home, Ryo happily watching me as I excitedly explained the sights along the journey.

I greeted the King and the Crown Prince with a smile on my face, making them happy. It had been too long since they last saw a smile on my face. It made Ryo smile as well, seeing how close I was to my family.

"Rui ge, I didn't know that you felt that way about men." Xiaofu softly stated, looking down in embarrassment. "I kept telling you how great those women looked, and yet you never swayed. I'm so sorry for not noticing."

"Xiaofu, it's alright. I didn't know either if I'm being honest. But all those moments in the past suddenly made sense the moment I realized." I replied, chuckling as I glanced at my lover, who was smiling and talking to Yixing about their nation's goods and prides.

"If he is the king, though, shouldn't he have a way to bear children?" He asked, making me look back to him. I saw he had a genuine concern for the nation I was married into, and it made me chuckle again.

"This is true, but we made an appointment of an official to help us adopt as many of the orphans in the country as we can. They will be the sons and daughters of the King, and they will be raised to take the throne when the time comes, just as we were." I explained, earning a smile from him as he jumped up and down, excited for my intentions.

"Edo is so much nicer of a country. They do not look down on such a relationship, but rather celebrate it?" He stated, giggling as I nodded in approval.

"I mean, I guess we don't necessarily call it a disgrace, but we do require a wife as well to make heirs." I looked to him in confusion, earning a chuckle from him. "I don't feel that way, but I read up on the laws of the land to become king, remember?"

"Ah, that," I replied, laughing.

I knew we both finally found happiness, and that our mother was smiling down on us from the heavens as she blessed us with peace.